# SUSI GREGG FOWLER

# Albertina, the Animals, and Me

## PICTURES BY JIM FOWLER

GREENWILLOW BOOKS
*An Imprint of HarperCollinsPublishers*

For Albertina's godmothers:
Nancy Warren Ferrell,
Jean Rogers, and Bridget Smith
Thanks, my writing friends — S. G. F.

For my niece and nephew,
Jennifer and Geoffrey Brand — J. F.

Watercolors were used to prepare the black-and-white art.
The text type is Kuenstler 480 BT.
Albertina, the Animals, and Me
Text copyright © 2000 by Susi Gregg Fowler
Illustrations copyright © 2000 by Jim Fowler
Printed in the United States of America.
For information address HarperCollins Children's Books,
a division of HarperCollins Publishers,
1350 Avenue of the Americas, New York, NY 10019.
www.harperchildrens.com

Library of Congress Cataloging-in-Publication Data

Fowler, Susi G.
Albertina, the animals, and me / by Susi Gregg Fowler ;
illustrated by Jim Fowler.
    p.    cm.
"Greenwillow Books."
Summary: When Molly and her best friend Albertina devise
a scheme to get a pet, everyone ends up surprised.
ISBN 0-688-17127-3 (trade)
ISBN 0-06-029160-5 (lib. bdg.)
[1. Pets—Fiction.    2. Best friends—Fiction.
3. Friendship—Fiction.]    I. Fowler, Jim, ill.    II. Title.
PZ7.F82975Ak    2000    [Fic]—dc21    99-41495    CIP

1  2  3  4  5  6  7  8  9  10    First Edition

# Contents

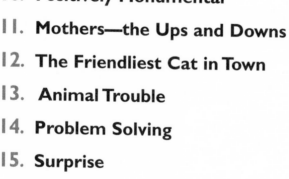

# Chapter 1

# Lonely

"I'm lonely," I said.

"Call Albertina," said Mom.

"I did. She's cleaning her room."

"What a kid," Mom said. She was probably wishing I was more like Albertina. Poor Mom.

"How about playing with your little brother awhile?" she suggested.

"Mom, Walter's a baby!"

"Well then, what about Violet?"

I shook my head. "She's still gone." Winter break was over, but Violet wouldn't be back for another week.

"Then call someone else. Clean your room. Read a book." Mom is a little like Albertina— always full of ideas. This time I didn't like any of them.

Something was missing from my life, and I knew what it was.

"Mom, I want a pet."

"You have a pet, Molly. You have Sylvia."

Sylvia is my goldfish. I'm fond of her, but let's face it. She's not cuddly. She can't chase a ball or a piece of string. She can't sleep at the foot of my bed. And she can't really comfort me when I'm lonely or sad. It's not her fault. She just doesn't have what you could call a sympathetic manner.

I didn't say all that to my mom. She's smart enough to figure it out herself. I just said, "I want a dog or cat. Please, Mom. Couldn't we go to the pound? We could surprise Dad and Walter."

"It would be a surprise, all right," Mom said.

"Come on, Mom," I pleaded. "I know you like cats. You used to have one."

"I did have a cat, a wonderful cat," she agreed. "But I married your dad, who is *not* fond of cats, and he's not going to change. That's the breaks, kiddo." My mom's sympathetic manner is not much better than Sylvia's.

"How about a dog, then?" I asked. "That would be even better."

"Oh, Molly. I don't have the energy to cope with a dog right now. Maybe in a couple of years, when your brother is older."

"I could die of loneliness by then," I said, feeling tears come. "Then you'll be sorry you couldn't be bothered."

"There's no point in crying," Mom said. "You can't always get what you want."

"Thanks a lot!" I cried. I grabbed my jacket and ran out of the house, slamming the door behind me. I knew I'd probably get in trouble for that, but I didn't care. I climbed up to the tree house Albertina and I had built, and I cried for a long time. Then I started getting cold, so I went back in the house.

"Can I go to the library, Mom?" I asked.

"*May* I," she corrected, "and yes, you may." I think she felt bad about saying no pets. She didn't even say anything about the door slamming. All she said was, "Maybe you should wash your face first, huh?"

I did, and then went to the library and checked out a book about caring for cats, one about raising a puppy, a book of animal stories, and a dog breed book. Maybe I couldn't have a pet, but I could read about them.

## Chapter 2

# Wishing and Hoping

"Molly, why don't you ever clean your room?" Albertina stumbled over my stack of library books.

"What are you, my mother?" I asked. "You don't make fun of my room and I won't make fun of yours."

"Touchy, touchy," Albertina said, laughing. Soon I started laughing, too. Albertina has that effect on me.

It's hard to believe that Albertina and I are so different about cleaning, since we're the same about most things. We think so much alike that sometimes we even say things at the same time. It drives my dad nuts.

Unfortunately, one of the ways we were alike was in not having pets.

"I told Mom I wanted a pet today," I said. "She acted as if Sylvia ought to be enough. No offense, Sylvia," I said, sprinkling some dried food into Sylvia's bowl, "but a fish is hardly the same as a dog."

"Or a cat," Albertina added. "I like cats better. I've told Daddy that most of my friends have pets, but he says that means I have plenty of pets to visit, so we don't need one cluttering up our house." She sighed. "I think life would be perfect if only I had a cat."

"I'd rather have a dog," I said, "but I'd settle for a cat."

"At least you have a goldfish, a brother, and *two* parents," Albertina reminded me. "I've only had my dad ever since I can remember."

Albertina's mother had died when she was little, but most of the time it doesn't seem to bother her. Suddenly I realized that if I could get lonely even with my family, it must be really hard for Albertina. "Are you lonely, Albertina?" I asked.

Albertina shrugged. "Sometimes I just wish I had someone besides my dad."

"You have me," I said, at the same time that she said, "I've got you." We laughed, but we both knew it wasn't really the same thing.

"You need a pet even more than I do," I said.

"We both need a pet," Albertina said. "So what are we going to do about it?"

"I don't know," I said. "We'll think of something." We sat around awhile until I started getting hungry. "Let's go see if Mom will give us a snack."

"How about these?" Mom suggested when we went down to the kitchen. "Your dad and I brought them home from dinner last night. There are three of them."

"Fortune cookies! Yes!" I said.

"Since Walter is napping and your dad is running, I think these were meant for us," Mom said. "Let's have some tea to go with them."

"Good idea." Albertina and I both agreed.

We sat at the table and Mom handed the plate of cookies to Albertina. "Guests first."

Albertina picked a cookie, broke it, and pulled out a yellow slip of paper.

"'Your dearest wish will come true.'" She looked at me. "Oh, Molly, I hope this is right!"

"Me, too," I said. "Now me. Hope it's as good as yours!"

"Well?" asked Albertina when I didn't say anything.

"That's strange," I said. "It's the same as

yours. Maybe they're all the same. What's the fun in that? Come on, Mom. Read yours."

"Here goes," she said. She groaned as she looked at the slip of paper.

"What does it say?" Albertina and I asked together.

"Mine is definitely different," Mom said with a sigh. "'Trouble is on the way.'" She looked at us. "Well, girls, I've been warned. Whatever you do, I'll be watching."

"You're the one who'd better be careful," Albertina said in a deep, scary voice. "You don't know our dearest wish. You only know whatever it is will come true."

"That's a scary thought," said Mom. "I don't want to think about it."

We laughed and finished our cookies and tea. Then Mom went to wake up Walter, and Albertina and I went back to my room to talk about wishes.

# Chapter 3

# Making Plans

"I bet we have the same dearest wish," I said. "Mine is for a pet—other than Sylvia."

Albertina turned pink. "Mine is for a pet or a mother," she confessed. "Do you think that's silly?" I shook my head. Imagine having to wish for a mother!

"If you really want a mother, what about that artist friend of your dad's?" I asked.

"Sally? Maybe. Daddy visited her last month, so I know he really likes her."

"But do *you* really like her?" I asked. "Would you want her for a mother?"

Albertina looked troubled. "I don't know. I

guess my first choice would be a cat—someone to cuddle in my lap. I'd tie colored ribbons around its neck and make it little cat toys."

"You couldn't do that with a mother," I said, and we both laughed.

"I don't really think I'll get a mom *or* a pet," Albertina said. "Daddy is pretty set in his ways. It's going to take more than a wish to change that. You'll have to share your cat with me."

I shook my head. "No cats. My dad doesn't like them."

"How do you know?"

"The way Dad feels about cats is no secret, believe me."

"But your mom likes them, right?" I nodded.

"She always had cats until she got Dad."

Albertina looked thoughtful. "Your dad's not allergic to cats, is he?" she asked.

"No. He just really dislikes them."

"Then tell him you'll keep it in your room,

the way Violet does with hers. Muffin never goes downstairs, even when Violet's door is open. Your dad wouldn't have to even see your cat."

I shook my head. "Dad's not going to change his mind. And Mom says a dog would be too much trouble, at least for now. I think our fortune cookies might be striking out."

"We can't make the fortune cookies do all the work. You need to stick with the cat idea," Albertina said, "and your dearest dream will come true. It'll work because deep down your

mom is already on your side. She just doesn't know it."

"If you say so," I said. "What's the plan?"

"First we find a cat, a truly irresistible cat. Maybe we could get one at the pound."

"That new girl at school, Mona, is volunteering there," I told Albertina. "She'd probably love to help."

"Good idea," said Albertina. "So then we bring this perfect cat to your house—"

"When my dad's not home," I interrupted.

"Right," said Albertina. "Your mom may be kind of businesslike on the outside, but she's pretty soft inside, and you know she loves cats. She won't be able to resist. What do you think?"

"I *think* we could be getting into a lot of trouble here," I said. "But I definitely think we should try. The fortune cookie *told* Mom trouble was on the way." Albertina laughed. We slapped our hands in a high five and went downstairs with big grins on our faces.

"What's with you girls?" my dad asked when he saw us. "You both look like the cat that swallowed the canary." At that we both laughed so hard we almost fell over.

Dad looked puzzled. "It wasn't *that* funny," he said.

"If you only knew," Albertina and I said at the very same time.

# Chapter 4

# The Trouble with Mona

Finding a cat turned out to be harder than we expected. Mona said you had to have your parents' permission to get a pound cat. So now we were reading want ads in the paper every night and checking bulletin boards around town.

Friday morning, Albertina whispered to me at our locker, "Meet me at lunch. I have something to tell you."

"About what?" I asked, hoping it had something to do with cats.

"It's about Mona," she whispered. "It's really weird."

Mona had just moved to town during winter break. I remembered how hard moving had been for me. I'd have been lost without Albertina. So Albertina and I decided *we* would be Mona's friends. It was easy, too. We liked her right away. We didn't know the rest of her family, but that didn't matter. Mona was the one we were interested in.

I sat down at my desk and looked over at Mona. She smiled at me. I sure couldn't see anything weird, except maybe her glasses, which are plaid. They weren't new, though. There's nothing strange about the way she acts. She plays the same games we do. She likes math and hates spelling. She's just a regular kid. What could Albertina be talking about?

Waiting for lunch was hard, but we knew better than to pass notes in Miss Aamot's class.

Finally, lunchtime arrived. "Well?" I asked when we sat down at the table.

"This morning I saw something odd through the window at Mona's," Albertina said in a low voice. "The something odd was Mona's mother. At least I think it was Mona's mother. All I saw were feet and legs. They were up in the air!"

"What are you talking about, Albertina?"

"Shhh," Albertina said, looking around. "Her feet were waving in the air, Molly. And listen. It gets worse. I was just leaving when I heard a terrible screech. Just as I turned around to see what it was, I saw curtains closing. Something is going on at that house." Weird. I had to admit it. "What was Mona's mother doing upside down?" Albertina went on. "That's no way for a mother to behave. Even I know that. And what was that loud cry? And what were they hiding? And why hasn't Mona told us anything about her family, anyway?"

"Maybe we haven't asked—" I started to say.

"Hush," Albertina whispered. "Here comes Mona."

"Hi. What's up?" she asked when she sat down. "What are you guys whispering about?" Albertina looked guilty. I wondered if I did.

"You look a little funny, Albertina," Mona said. "Are you okay?"

"*I'm* fine," Albertina said. "How about *you*, Mona? Anything unusual in your life?"

"Nope," Mona answered, and took out her lunch. Albertina gave me a look that said it was my turn to say something. I was just about to ask Mona to tell us about her family when she opened a plastic container full of little brown chunks of something.

"What *is* that?" I asked, pointing. I couldn't help myself. It looked awful!

"Who knows?" Mona sounded cheerful enough. I looked at Albertina and could tell she was thinking the same thing I was. Mona held a forkful of whatever it was up to her nose and sniffed. "Flynn likes experimenting."

"Flynn?"

"That's my mom. She calls recipes cooking spells." Albertina looked at me and raised her eyebrows.

"Not bad," said Mona, tasting the jiggly little squares. "Tofu, I think. Want a bite?"

I tried not to shudder. "Thanks, anyway," I said.

Albertina looked green. "I think I'll go eat with Sam and Flora," she said.

I unwrapped my peanut butter sandwich. It looked a lot better than usual. Maybe I'd quit complaining about Dad's lunches. Poor Mona.

# Chapter 5

# Mona's Terrible Mother

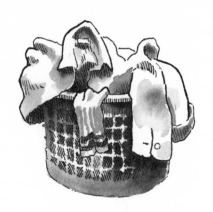

"Hey, Mona!" I ran to catch up with her after school. "Do you want to come over?"

"I need to ask my mom," she said. "Let's stop by my house first."

Yes! Now I'd really get the goods on Mona's mother.

"I'm home, Flynn," she yelled as we walked in the door. I stared. I'd never seen a house that looked like Mona's. The whole place was a mess! Books and papers were piled everywhere. Even the couch was covered. This wasn't a room *my* mother would find acceptable. I felt a little sorry for Mona. Then again, maybe *her* mom didn't nag her about keeping her room clean.

Mona opened the back door and went outside. "Flynn!"

"I'm in the shed," her mom called back.

"I'll go see if we can come out," Mona told me. "You wait here."

"Can't I come out with you?"

Mona shook her head. "No one's allowed in the backyard unless Flynn okays it."

Stranger and stranger. It gave me a chance to look around the house, though.

Arghh! I bet I jumped back a couple of feet. There on the dining-room table, someone had spread out a pile of bones. Some centerpiece!

Mona walked in and found me staring and poking at the bones. "Flynn's into bones," she said. "These are an owl's. She's cleaned them and now she's putting them together."

"Should I go meet her?" I asked, wondering if I really wanted to.

Mona shook her head. "Some other time, Molly."

"Fine with me," I said, but what I thought was, What is it with Mona's mother? What's she hiding? My mom and dad practically fall all over themselves, they're so eager to meet my friends. If Mona's mother wasn't interested in me, maybe it wasn't any big deal. It wasn't a point in her favor, though.

"I can go," Mona said. "Do you want to see my room first?" I did, of course, so we went upstairs. We passed laundry baskets full of clothes, piles of rags, boxes full of notebooks, and all kinds of other stuff.

"Do you have a big family?" I asked.

"Nope. Just me and my mom and stepdad," she said. "My dad's in Texas, where we used to live. Looks like a family of ten lives here, huh?"

I didn't know what to say.

There weren't any tofu snacks or old bones in Mona's room. It looked like any kid's room, except for Albertina's, of course. Mona's mother might be odd, but Mona was just a normal kid.

"Want a snack before we go to your house?" Mona asked.

I shook my head, remembering her lunch. "Dad will wonder where I am."

As we came down the stairs, a strange cry sounded from outside, like something from a horror movie. I grabbed Mona's arm.

"Don't worry, Molly. You'll get used to it," she said. I didn't think so, but before I could ask what was going on, I looked out the back-door window and saw something that stopped the words in my throat. Mona's mother! It had to be Mona's mother, but she didn't look like any mother I'd ever seen.

She wore bright purple pants and a baggy coat. Huge leather gloves reached up to her elbows, and her long, fuzzy brown hair blew around her head like a dark cloud. She turned toward the window, and I blinked to make sure what I was seeing was real. An owl, a real live owl with big yellow eyes, rested on her arm—and the two of them stared straight at me. Mona's mother bent down and said something and the owl turned its head away. A witch! Cross my heart, Mona's mother looked exactly like a witch. No wonder Mona didn't explain things!

"Mona, let's go," I croaked when my voice started working again.

Mona waved out the window just as if her mother wasn't— well, whatever she was—and we left. I had a million questions for Mona, but I was too shocked to ask any of them.

Molly, get a grip, I told myself.

I didn't believe in witches. I knew that. Even if I did believe in witches, I didn't believe they'd have kids—not nice, normal kids like Mona. So witches were out. That was better. I mean, really—witches! Sometimes I scare myself.

Mona chattered all the way to my house, which was fine with me. I was busy thinking. If Mona's mother wasn't a witch, and of course she wasn't, then what was it with her? She was weird, right? Her kid called her by her first name. She stood on her head. She was hiding things in her backyard. Something around her house screamed a lot. She kept bones on the dining-room table. And she had a very strange pet. I shivered. I was glad I didn't have to live with her. What did Mona really think about her? What did *I* really think? I needed to talk to Albertina.

# Chapter 6

# Home
# Sweet Home

"I'm home," I called as we walked in the door and I dropped my backpack on the hall table.

"Walter and I are in the kitchen, making cookies," Dad hollered back. I stuck my head into the kitchen.

"I'll be back in a little while. I'm going out to the tree house," I said. I turned and asked Mona, "Okay with you? You can meet Dad and Walter later."

"Fine," she said. "Tell me about your dad. Why isn't he at work?"

"He works at home and takes care of my little brother, Walter," I explained. "That's a lot more work now that Walter can walk. Lately he's been making cookies a lot so Walter can stir."

"Nice dad," Mona said.

I nodded. "The only bad thing about him is that he won't let me get a cat, and my mom won't let me get a dog—at least not now."

"Too bad," said Mona. "Flynn says pets are really important." I bet she does, I thought.

"Wow, you and Albertina did all this?" Mona asked when she saw the tree house.

"With a little help from my grandfather," I said. I know showing off isn't supposed to be very nice, but I couldn't help being proud of what we'd done. Mona noticed all our special touches, too.

"This is so great, Molly!" She was definitely our kind of kid, no matter what her mom was like.

We stayed out in the tree house until we started getting cold.

"Let's go see how those cookies are coming,"
I said.

"Perfect timing," Dad said as we walked in.
He was wiping up the counter after all Walter's
help. I introduced him to Mona.

"And this is my little brother, Walter," I said.

Walter sat in his high chair, squealing
cheerfully. "Cookie!" Most of his cookie stuck
to his fingers and face, with a little milk mixed
in just to make it spread better.

He held up his arms. "Hugs." I looked at his hands and face again.

"No way," I said under my breath.

"Oh, Molly. He's so cute. You're so lucky." Mona bent down close to him. He reached out one sticky little hand and grabbed her shirtsleeve.

"Bad move, Mona," I said. I knew enough to keep my distance. You can always tell the kids who don't have little brothers or sisters.

"He looks kind of different from you, Molly," Mona said with a question in her voice.

"He's from China," I said. "We adopted him

when he was just a few months old."

"Down!" This time Walter commanded.

"Would you clean him up and get him out of his chair, Molly?" Dad asked.

I sighed. "See how much work babies are, Mona? Consider yourself lucky." But I cleaned Walter up, got him out of his chair, and gave him a big hug. I *do* love him, and I figure he's *much* better than a big brother would be.

"No Albertina today?" Dad asked.

"She'll be over later," I said. "She stayed after school to help Miss Aamot clean the turtle tank."

"So, Mona," Dad said, "tell me about yourself."

"Not now, Dad," I interrupted before Mona could say anything. I knew I was being rude, but I was scared of what she might tell him about her mother. He might get so worried he wouldn't let me go to her house. No, Albertina and I needed to find out what was going on first. Then we'd tell our parents.

"Let's go to my room," I said, ignoring Dad's frown and Mona's surprised look. "Just tell Albertina to come to my room, would you?" I asked him. "Please," I added. He nodded.

"I like your dad," Mona said.

Of course she likes him, I thought. He doesn't stand on his head before breakfast or walk around with owls on his arm. He uses plain old recipes, not cooking spells. He doesn't hide in the backyard with things that scream, unless you count my little brother.

"You'd like my dad, too," she continued. "He's a lot of fun. That's the worst part about moving— being so far away from him."

I looked at her. It had been hard enough for me to move across town. Mona had moved from a completely different state, away from her friends and her own dad. I didn't care what Mona's mother was. I was going to be Mona's friend, and that was that.

# Chapter 7

# Suspicions

"Hey, what's up, you guys?" Albertina raced into the room, pigtails flying. "Want to go to the tree house?"

"Too cold," I answered. "We've already been out there."

"Then let's go to the library," Albertina said. "We could start our projects on the states."

"Albertina's the only kid I know who doesn't wait until the last minute to do homework," I told Mona. "My mom keeps hoping some of Albertina's good sense will rub off on me."

"It hasn't," Albertina and I said at the very same time.

Mona laughed. "You two," she said. "It's almost spooky."

I could think of spookier things.

"Too bad you don't have your cat yet," Albertina said.

Mona looked confused. "I thought your dad wouldn't let you get a cat," she said.

"He won't," I said.

"Your dearest wish will come true," Albertina said. "Don't forget."

"I'm confused," said Mona, so we explained about the fortune cookies.

"I hope you *both* get cats," Mona said. "I sure love mine."

"What's he like?" Albertina and I asked.

"There you go, talking like twins again," Mona said. "He's a big, black cat—a perfect witch's cat." Great. "His name is Creeps," she added—which was exactly what this gave me.

"That reminds me, I'd better be getting home

now," Mona said. "Creeps will be hungry, and I need to help Flynn with our dinner, too. Thanks for showing me the tree house, Molly."

As soon as Mona left, I told Albertina everything I'd learned about Mona and her mother.

"What do you think it means?" Albertina asked. "She *seems* like such a nice kid."

"She *is* a nice kid," I said. "It's her mom who's the problem. So what do we do?"

"You should have just asked her," Albertina said. "I'll do it tomorrow."

"Don't!" I said. "Whatever Mona's mother

is, it's something strange. You can't just ask."

"Then we'll have to get to know her better," Albertina said.

"Who? Mona?" I asked.

"No, silly," said Albertina. "Mona's mother."

I didn't like the idea. Albertina had seen Mona's mother's feet; I'd seen the rest.

"We need another plan. How about an overnight?" Albertina suggested. "Mona would love it."

I groaned. "Albertina, I can't." Albertina knows I'm a teeny bit scared of the dark, especially in strange places. Mona's house definitely counted as strange.

"Couldn't we just go for dinner instead?" I asked.

It was Albertina's turn to groan. "That's going too far, Molly. Remember Mona's lunch?"

"Right," I agreed.

"There's only one thing to do," Albertina

said. Another plan was on the way. "We must become spies."

Spies. I liked it! "Now?"

Albertina shook her head. "It'll be dark soon. Our parents wouldn't like it." Neither would I, come to think of it, but I didn't say so.

"Besides, we need to dress for spy work," Albertina said.

"How do spies dress?" I asked.

"Think, Molly. Dark clothes, sunglasses, hats you pull down low—disguise."

"Won't people think we look a little peculiar?" I asked.

"Who cares? We'll be in disguise. No one will know it's us."

"What will we do?"

"We'll sneak around and peek in the windows," Albertina said. "Then we'll check out the backyard."

"Not the backyard. Someone will see us!" By someone, I meant Mona's mother.

"Mr. Bonk lives behind Mona's," Albertina said. "We'll spy from his yard. Even if he catches us, he won't be mad. Maybe he'll be at school, anyway." Mr. Bonk is our gym teacher.

"On Saturday?" I asked. "I'm not worried about being caught by Mr. Bonk, anyway. It's Mona's mother who worries me."

"Maybe she'll have something else going on."

"Like what? A witches' convention?" I asked. Albertina laughed and so did I, but not very hard.

We were both a little nervous, but at least we had a plan.

# Chapter 8

# Spies!

"Expecting rain, Albertina?" Dad asked when she showed up Saturday morning wearing her dad's raincoat. "Or are you just preparing for every possibility?" Albertina peered at him over her sunglasses.

"How did he recognize me?" Albertina asked as we headed for Mona's.

"Sixth sense," I said, taking my sunglasses out of my pocket and pulling my hat down. "Let's get to work."

One moment we were standing on the

sidewalk outside Mona's house. The next thing I knew, Albertina's face was pressed up against a window. She motioned me over.

"What is *wrong* with you?" I squawked when I reached her. "What if someone sees you? What will you say?"

"Molly. Disguise-a your voice. Someone might-a hear you."

I started to giggle. Albertina glared at me. "Shhhh."

"I can't help it. You sound like that Italian restaurant commercial."

"I'm-a trying to sound-a like-a someone besides-a myself. I suggest-a you do-a the same. Now, what-a part of the house is-a thees?" I had to bite my tongue to keep from laughing. But then I remembered what we were doing, and that stopped the laugh right in my throat.

"We *can't* just look in their windows, Albertina," I said.

"Well, you can't spy without looking at something," Albertina scowled, forgetting her accent. "We're not exactly invisible just standing around on the sidewalk, either," she added. She had a point. "So, what-a room-a is-a thees?" she asked again.

"I think that's the living room. See, way over there, the table with all the books?"

"Okay. Wow! This is just like your room, Molly. What a mess!"

"Thanks," I said. "What happened to your accent?"

"Too hard to keep it up," Albertina said.

"Good," I said. "Now what do we do?"

"We look in the other windows, of course." I didn't like this, but Albertina was right. If we didn't look, we weren't going to see anything. Besides, even though spying was a little scary, it sure beat spending the night or eating dinner at Mona's. We sneaked through tall grass and weeds as we moved around the house, window by window.

"Okay. Here's the kitchen," Albertina said. "I don't see any newts or toads or eyeballs."

"Yuck, Albertina. Don't say things like that."

As we edged around the house, we came to a tall fence. We couldn't see through it. "I'm not trying to climb this," I said. Albertina agreed.

"Mr. Bonk's," she whispered.

We went back to the sidewalk and around the block until we came to Mr. Bonk's. We crept through his yard until we came to a huge hedge between his house and Mona's.

"It's almost as tall as the fence," Albertina said. "Maybe we can look through it."

But the hedge was thick and prickly. We couldn't see anything. "It's like the thorns around Sleeping Beauty's castle," Albertina whispered. "Maybe it's magic."

"Very funny, Albertina. We need to find out what's going on in that yard. Let me climb up on your shoulders."

I barely got my head over the hedge when I saw something that sent me tumbling off Albertina and sent my sunglasses flying.

"Well?" asked Albertina.

"It's Mona's mother all right," I said. "She's got hold of something awful—all I can see are scaly legs and claws."

"What is it?" asked Albertina.

"I don't know. It's big and it's on the ground on some kind of leash or something. I can't see very well. Oh, Albertina, it has wings—it's almost like a dragon!"

"This I've got to see," said Albertina. "Hold

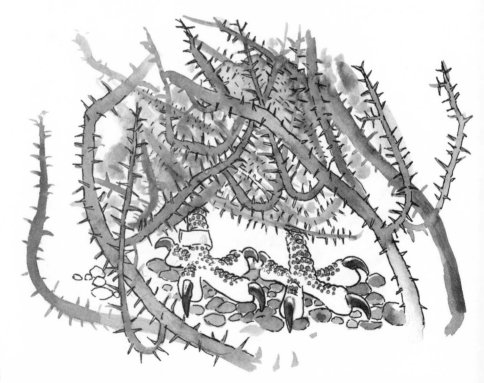

still." She took off her coat and started crawling up my back, but before she reached the top of the hedge, we heard a shriek. Albertina froze as something rustled against the other side of the hedge. She poked her head up over the hedge. "I can see the back of her head," she whispered. "So that's Mona's mother."

"It's not the tooth fairy," I said. "Hurry up. You're hurting my shoulders."

"I can't see what she's got," Albertina said. "Oh, wow!"

"What is it?" I said. "Tell me." But before she did, we heard a voice.

"There you go, my pretty." There was another screech—but I think this one came from Albertina. The next thing I knew, Albertina was on the ground. "My pretty?" we mouthed at each other, not sure whether to laugh or cry.

And then we heard Mona's mother. "Is someone there?"

# Chapter 9

# Caught

"Wait right there," Mona's mother said. I froze.

It was probably the worst moment of my life. Before I could make my feet move, I heard something click in the hedge. There was a gate hidden in all that brush. Mona's mother appeared, and now it was too late for escape.

"May I help you?" she asked.

"Is Mona home?" I croaked.

"She's helping at the animal shelter," said Mona's mother. "Do you girls want to come in?"

"No," I blurted out.

"No, thank you," said Albertina, whose good manners never failed her. "I'm Albertina and this is Molly."

"I'm Flynn," she said, "Mona's mother." She pointed at me. "I've seen you before." She seemed to be waiting for me to say something, but my mouth wasn't working.

"What are you doing out here?" Albertina asked Mona's mother. "And what was that animal—and where is it now?"

I gasped. Albertina goes straight to the point, I've got to admit.

"She's a golden eagle. I took her back to the shed. I'm afraid she'll never fly again, but I exercise her every day. You never know."

"What about the bird I saw the other day?" I asked, finally getting my voice back.

"The short-eared owl? We call him Mo. A guy from Fish and Wildlife brought him over when I first got to town. He'll be fine, I think.

He just needs a little time to recover."

"But why are they here?" Albertina asked.

Mona's mother looked surprised. "Didn't Mona tell you? I'm a wildlife biologist. I have a permit to work with injured birds. I take care of them and release them when they're well again. If they can't be released, we find homes for them in educational programs."

"I've never seen such a big bird before," I said. "It didn't even look like a bird to me. I didn't know what I was seeing."

"Scary, huh?" Flynn laughed, but it was a nice laugh. "You do have to be careful of her—and the others. That's why I wear these big gloves," she said, "and, of course, it's why the backyard is off limits. The birds don't mean harm, of course, but wild creatures deserve some privacy and distance from people."

"You are a very interesting woman, Flynn," said Albertina.

"Why, thank you," said Mona's mother.

"You do headstands, don't you?" Albertina asked.

Flynn laughed. "Guilty. I do yoga most mornings. Helps keep my head clear. Has Mona been telling tales about her strange mother?"

"Mona never said a word," Albertina said. "I saw you one morning—or I saw your feet. I never knew a mother who stood on her head. And then I heard these strange noises. They were the birds, I guess, but they sounded like

screams to me. Later, Molly came over, and saw
you with the owl—with Mo—and there were
other peculiar things about your house. You
seemed odd, I guess. We didn't know what to
think—and we were worried about Mona."

Albertina believes in saying what she means,

even if it's embarrassing. I could feel myself blush, and I was afraid to look at Flynn.

But Flynn started laughing. She laughed and laughed, and her laugh was a lot like Albertina's. After a while, it was impossible not to join in. "I guess I am a trifle odd," she said when she finally caught her breath, "but I'm harmless enough. Being the way I am suits me—and it seems to suit Mona. I'm glad Mona has friends who are looking out for her—and I hope you'll be able to get used to my strange ways."

"I look forward to it," Albertina said seriously.

"We'd better be getting home," I said. "Please tell Mona we were here."

"Don't forget your sunglasses," Flynn said, picking up the pair I'd dropped in panic.

I gulped. "Thanks."

"Good-bye," Flynn called after us. "Next time, feel free to come to the front door."

Albertina and I blushed at the very same time.

## Chapter 10

# Positively
# Monumental

"Don't say anything, Albertina," I said as we headed home. "Not one word." She didn't *say* anything, but she did start to laugh, and after a while, so did I.

"Mom always says I'm too quick to jump to conclusions," I said.

"Nobody could say there's anything wrong with your imagination, though," Albertina said. "I'm the one who started it anyway, so it's not all your fault. What do you think of Flynn?"

I thought I was glad my mom wasn't quite as full of surprises as Mona's, but I had to admit that a mother who took care of wounded birds was pretty neat.

"I promised I'd keep Walter entertained for a couple of hours today," I said. "Want to help?"

"I think I'll go see if Violet is back from her trip," Albertina said. "Maybe we'll come over later."

We said good-bye, and I headed for home.

Between spying on Mona's mother and playing with my brother, I was exhausted. I got into my pajamas soon after dinner that night and was poring over a book called *Grooming Your Cat*, when the phone rang.

"Molly! I've got to talk to you," someone whispered over the line. "Can I come over?"

"Albertina, is that you? I can hardly hear you."

"Of course it's me. Can I come? Now? I'll tell my dad you invited me to spend the night."

"What's going on?" I asked—not that it mattered, of course. Albertina doesn't need a reason to come over.

"I can't tell you right now," she said. "That's why I have to come over."

"I'll check," I said. "Hold on.

"You can come," I said after I got the okay. "What's the big deal? Give me a hint."

"I can't," she said, whispering again, "but it's something positively monumental."

"Hurry up, then," I said, and hung up.

I went into the kitchen to make a snack and

wait for her. It wasn't long before she rushed in the back door.

"Molly!" She grabbed me. "Thank goodness you're here." Where did she think I'd be?

"Well?" I asked.

"Upstairs. Please," Albertina said. "Hurry."

We went to my room, where Albertina flopped onto my bed.

"Oh, Molly, I don't know what to do," she said. "I'm miserable."

"What? What is going on?" I was definitely losing patience.

"You don't have to scream," Albertina said. She looked as if she was going to cry.

I tried to speak calmly. "Albertina. Tell me what is going on or I *will* scream."

"Okay. You know how my dad says, 'Take care what you wish or it might come true'? Well, you remember my wish, my dearest wish?"

"Duh," I said. What did she think?

She took a deep breath. "My dad and Sally are thinking about getting married!" For a moment I couldn't think of *what* to say. "My gosh, Albertina. Did he just tell you?"

"He *didn't* tell me," Albertina said. "He hasn't said a word about anything except Duke."

"I'm lost. Duke?"

Albertina sighed. "Sally's bringing Duke to stay with us."

"Who's Duke? Her son?"

"Don't be silly, Molly. Duke is her dog."

"A mother *and* a pet? Wow. That must have been some fortune cookie. It's everything you wanted!"

"Except I'm the one who wanted a cat," Albertina reminded me, "and I'm not sure that I want either one of them now."

"Wait a minute. How do you know they're getting married if your dad didn't tell you?"

"Because of Duke," Albertina said.

"I don't understand what Duke has to do with it," I said.

Albertina took a deep breath. "Sally is going to France for a month. She begged Daddy to take Duke so he doesn't have to stay at the kennel. I think she's seeing if Duke likes us enough for her to marry Daddy, and Daddy's finding out if he can stand Duke enough to marry Sally. It's the only reason he'd ever agree to this. I know my dad. He doesn't like dogs, and he especially doesn't like this dog. Trust me. This is a test."

"Some people have all the luck," I said. "I wish somebody would bring a dog to my house. If you're lucky and they get married, you'll have a dog forever!"

"This is about more than getting a pet," Albertina said in a small voice. "I'm scared, Molly. This could change my life forever."

I didn't know what to say.

## Chapter 11

# Mothers— the Ups and Downs

"Albertina, why don't you just talk to your dad about this?" I asked. Albertina is usually what my mom calls straightforward.

"I can't," Albertina said. "He's acting so strange. I've never seen him like this."

I'd never seen *Albertina* like this, either. I figured it was my job to cheer her up. "Well, at least it will be fun to have a dog. And mothers have their good points, too."

I thought that would make her laugh, but she didn't even smile.

"I'm going to go brush my teeth," she said.

When she came back, she was ready to talk again. "I *think* I like Sally," she said. "In fact, I *do* like Sally, but I don't know if I want her for a mother."

"How bad could she be?" I asked.

"Molly. She could be horrible. You never had to think about your mother, never had to decide whether you'd pick her or not."

I nodded. "Yeah. I just got stuck with her."

Albertina laughed a little. "This could change everything with me and Daddy. What if Sally tries to change the rules on me? What if she tries to make me eat things I hate? What if she doesn't like my friends?"

"No sweat, Albertina," I said. "Well, maybe you might have to worry about Violet and Mona, but she's sure to love me."

At least she really laughed this time.

"Tell me about Sally's dog," I said.

"Daddy doesn't have much good to say about him, but of course he doesn't like anything that makes a mess. You know what a neatnik he is."

I did. I knew someone who was a lot like him, too, but I didn't say so.

"Daddy says Duke is spoiled," Albertina went on. "He yaps constantly, which gives Daddy a headache. He sits on the furniture. He sheds so badly that huge clumps of dog hair fly everywhere and even the butter gets covered with dog hair."

"Yuck!" I said. "Your dad is really letting this dog stay with you? He's the guy who said a cat would be too much trouble."

Albertina nodded. "That's why I'm so sure they're thinking about marriage. This is *not* just a simple dog-sitting job, Molly."

"I see what you mean. When will they be here?"

"Monday night," said Albertina.

"Yikes! Then I guess you'd better decide pretty fast whether you want to make friends with him or not, right?"

"And whether I want a mother or not," said Albertina.

Neither of us slept much that night.

## Chapter 12

# The Friendliest Cat in Town

Getting up Sunday morning was hard, but Albertina's dad was expecting her and I had Sunday school. We agreed to go for a walk later. "I'll invite Mona, too," Albertina said.

We met at Albertina's at three o'clock. "Don't be too late," her dad said when we left. "We need to get ready for tomorrow." Albertina groaned.

We stopped at the grocery store to buy some gum.

"Molly, come look at this!" Albertina called.

She pointed out a sign reading OWNERS MOVING. NEED NEW HOME FOR THE FRIENDLIEST CAT IN TOWN. CALL JACK OR HILDA ANDERSON.

"I know her," said Albertina, practically jumping up and down. "She worked in my dad's office. They live right next to the library."

"What are we waiting for?" asked Mona. "This could be it, Molly—your very own cat!"

My heart pounded and my mouth felt dry. I knew this could get me in a lot of trouble. But it wouldn't hurt to look, would it?

We knocked, and Hilda Anderson answered the door. "Albertina, what a pleasant surprise," she said. She was even more pleased when she found out why we were there.

"This is Sam," she said as she picked up a large orange cat and put him in my arms. Sam curled up under my chin and began purring. I was in love.

"He's perfect," said Albertina. "No true cat lover could resist him."

"Why don't you call your parents?" Ms. Anderson asked.

I took a big gulp. "No, thank you. My mom really wants a cat." I hoped I was right.

Ms. Anderson wrote down her name and phone number. "Just in case," she said. Sam was licking my cheek now. Why shouldn't I keep him? After all, Albertina's wish was working out, even if she had second thoughts.

"Thank goodness it's Sunday and Mom's home," I said as we headed for home.

But Mom looked as shocked as Dad when I walked in.

"This is Sam," I said nervously. "His family is moving. He needs a new place to live."

"I hate cats!" my father said.

"I'd better go now," Albertina said. "Coming with me, Mona?" I was on my own.

"The lady said he's the friendliest cat in town," I tried again, hoping to get Dad to smile. "Look at him—he's huge and beautiful. I think his eyes are the same color as yours, Dad."

"You have to admit he is a handsome cat," Mom said.

"I don't have to admit anything of the sort," said Dad.

Mom held Walter so he could pet Sam. He squealed with delight—Walter, not the cat.

"Walter likes him," Mom said. "But I'm very

disappointed in you, Molly." My heart sank. "He's here now, though, so I don't see why we couldn't give it a try. He *does* seem very friendly."

Dad made a face. "Do I get a vote?"

"How about a one-week trial?" Mom suggested. "Cats are independent creatures," she said to my dad. "You'll hardly know he's in the house."

Sometimes Mom gets things wrong.

That first night, a horrible scream woke us all up. It came from my parents' room.

I ran to the room. "Take him," Mom said, handing me a cranky-looking Sam. "That shriek was your father. This is not a good beginning, Molly."

"I guess Sam is used to sleeping with people," I said.

"Well, your father is *not* used to sleeping with cats," Mom said.

"Bad move, Sam," I scolded, carrying him

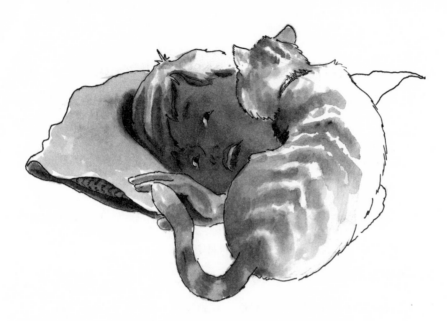

back to my room. "You sleep with me."

At breakfast the next day, Sam climbed up in Dad's lap.

"Get him off me," Dad growled. I tried, but Sam dug his claws into Dad's leg.

"Yiiiii!" Dad jumped up, spilling his coffee and burning his hand. Sam rolled onto the floor and Dad tripped over him as he hurried to the sink to run cold water over his hand.

"Ouch!" He bumped against the table and spilled everybody's orange juice. Sam yowled.

"Poor Sam!" Mom and I both said.

"Poor Sam!" said Dad. "What about poor Dad?"

He threw his hands up in the air and left the room.

"I hope this wasn't a mistake," Mom said, wiping up the orange juice.

"Dad's bound to get used to him, he's such a friendly cat," I said. "Don't worry, Mom."

"Remember, it's just a trial," Mom said. "Try to keep him in your room, okay?" She looked toward the door. "I wish I didn't have to go to work today." She looked so worried I could tell she was on our side.

Albertina ran in a few minutes later. "Hi, Sam," she said, stroking my cat, who greeted her like an old friend. "I wish I was getting a cat. Tonight I meet the dreaded Duke."

"It could be fun, Albertina," I told her.

She didn't look convinced.

# Chapter 13

# Animal Trouble

I couldn't wait to get home after school, but it was my day to help Miss Aamot after class. Mom was already home from work when I ran in the front door. She frowned.

"I don't know what happened, but Sam got out of your room. Guess who got tripped while he was making dinner? This is not the way to win over your dad, Molly."

"I'm sorry," I said. "Do you think Sam can stay anyhow?"

"It's been a bit of a disaster so far," she said,

"but tonight will probably be better."

She was wrong again.

After dinner Dad said, "I need a break," and went into the other room to read the paper.

*Yowl!* The shriek brought both Mom and me running.

This time the scream wasn't Dad's. Sam glared at Dad from under the piano, his hair standing out like orange dandelion fuzz.

"He was in my chair!" said Dad.

"Poor Sam," I said, scooping up the upset cat.

"I didn't sit on him on purpose."

"You sat on him?" Mom reached over and patted Sam. "Poor thing. Take him to your room, Molly. I'd better get back to Walter." My little brother was doing some yowling of his own in the kitchen.

As I carried Sam past my dad, he made a funny noise.

"He growled at me!" Dad said.

"He's scared," I said.

"More like mad," Dad said. "He sure doesn't look very friendly to me." He had a point.

I put the cat in my room, closed the window, shut the door, and went back into the kitchen.

"How will they learn to like each other if we keep them apart all the time?" I asked.

Mom shrugged. "This experiment may fail, Molly. I told you your dad is not a cat person." What did that mean, anyway? I was about to ask Mom when the phone interrupted me.

"Hello," I said.

"They're here," Albertina whispered.

"Really, Albertina," I said crossly. "These whispered calls are getting to be a bad habit."

"Why don't you just drop by?" she whispered some more.

Before I could answer, she hung up—but not before I heard the sound of shrill barking.

"Okay if I stop by Albertina's for a while?" I asked.

"Be home by seven thirty, okay?" Mom said. "Make sure the cat's locked up before you go."

I checked on Sam one more time and then headed for Albertina's.

"Hi," I said when Albertina's father came to the door. But before he even had a chance to greet me, something gray and fuzzy streaked past me. Oops. I'd just met Duke.

Albertina's father raced down the block yelling, "Duke! Duke!"

Albertina came running out. "Oh, no!" Soon we were all three chasing Sally's dog. He suddenly stopped.

"Nice dog, good Duke," Albertina's father gasped, reaching for the dog's collar. Just as he reached it, Duke started running again. This time he ran in circles around us, always just out of reach. Albertina's dad turned red, and I heard him say something Albertina and I would have gotten in trouble for. He was really mad.

Finally I got an idea. I sat down on the ground. Duke came right over and sat in my lap. He stuck his pointy little snout up in my face and licked me.

"He likes you!" Albertina said as she came closer.

"Good job, Molly," said Albertina's dad, grabbing hold of the dog's collar. "Now. Back in the house with you. Sally's only been gone half an hour and you're already causing trouble."

Duke hung his head. I felt kind of bad, as if I'd tricked him. Well, I had. But when we got back in the house, he still seemed to like me. He followed me right up to Albertina's room.

"No, Duke," said Albertina and closed the door in his face.

"Can't he come in?" I asked.

Albertina shook her head. "He's too wild. I'm afraid he'll break things." Albertina does have a lot of beautiful, breakable things. The truth is, I'm always afraid *I'll* knock them over.

Then the trouble started. "*Woooooo, woooo,*"

Duke began. Next he started barking louder and louder. Finally he started scratching the door, and soon we heard the doorknob rattling. Albertina opened the door a crack. "Bad dog!" she yelled. "Gross! He had the doorknob in his mouth!"

Duke bolted past her and into the room. He leaped onto my lap again, knocking over Albertina's bed table as he came.

"It's the end of life as we know it," Albertina groaned.

"I don't know, Albertina. He seems pretty sweet to me."

"That's because you don't have to live with him, Molly. This dog is crazy!"

"He's just a dog, Albertina. What do you expect?"

"I expect to be able to walk in the door without someone attacking me. I expect to be able to leave my bedroom door open without fear of total destruction. That's what I expect."

"Don't listen to her, Duke," I said, scratching behind his ears.

"Imagine what he'll do tomorrow when Dad goes to work and I go to school. Sally doesn't leave until Wednesday, but she can't keep Duke at her sister's, so the dog-sitting has begun. Daddy says I have to come straight home from school every day and walk the dog."

"But that'll be fun, Albertina," I said. "I'll help."

"You're a real friend, Molly. Thanks."

"No problem," I said. "I like dogs."

"Dogs like you, too," said Albertina. "I can see that. Too bad *your* dad's not thinking about marrying Sally."

"Albertina!" I said. "What would my mother say?"

"I was just teasing," Albertina said. "But I do wish Duke was staying at your house."

"Me, too," I said. "Sam's not working out too well so far."

"He will," Albertina said. "You'll see. You're so lucky, Molly. If Daddy marries Sally, that's it. I'll have nothing but a crazy dog for the rest of my life."

As much as I liked Sam, I couldn't think of anything better than having a dog, even a crazy one. I guess that just shows that best friends don't always like the same things.

# Chapter 14

# Problem Solving

I went to bed, but I couldn't get to sleep. I kept thinking how tonight both Albertina and I had pets, and just a few days ago all there'd been was Sylvia. Sam curled up next to me. It was very comforting. "It's not your fault you're not a dog," I said. "You're a very sweet cat."

The next day after school I went home with Albertina. The coffee table was knocked over and there was dog slobber on the window where Duke had been watching for someone to come home.

"Yuck," said Albertina. She certainly wasn't enjoying this dog. I put Duke on the leash, and we went out for a walk around the neighborhood. I could tell this was a lot more fun for me than it was for Albertina.

When I got home, Dad was making dinner. "Your cat yowled off and on all day," he complained.

"He was lonely, Dad. He's such a friendly cat. He doesn't like staying in his room."

"What happened to 'cats are independent creatures'?" Dad asked. I ran up to my room and Sam met me at the door, rubbing against my leg and meowing. I tied a crumpled piece of paper to a string and dragged it around the floor while he leaped around, pouncing on it and then chasing it again. It wasn't quite like walking a dog, but he was still good company.

When Dad called me to set the table, I carefully closed the door again. I heard Sam

batting at the door from the other side. "Sorry,"
I said.

"Got to keep you and Dad apart." Sighing, I
went downstairs.

After dinner I went back to my room to read
a while and be with Sam. I could hear Mom and
Dad in the living room. The fact that I could hear
their voices clear upstairs wasn't a good sign.

Awhile later, I heard footsteps on the stairs
and Mom's knock on my door. I knew she was
coming to tell me they'd decided we had to get
rid of Sam. I clutched him to my chest.

"A week's trial! You promised!" I blurted out
when she walked in.

She put a pile of clothes on my bed. "I'm just

delivering laundry," she said, but she looked upset. "You'll get your week, Molly, but you need to be prepared for the possibility that your dad won't change his mind. He's pretty upset with you for springing this on us. He's right, you know."

"I'm sorry, Mom," I said. "I just wanted a pet so badly."

She sat down on the edge of the bed and put an arm around me. Sam stretched out a lazy paw and rested it on her leg. She scratched his neck. "You need to cooperate, you rascal." Albertina was right about Mom being on our side, but I knew that if it came to a choice between Sam and Dad, Dad was a sure winner— at least as far as Mom went.

I need a plan, I thought after Mom left. In order to keep my pet, it was going to have to be a really *good* plan. So I did what I always do when I have a problem. I called Albertina.

"She's at Mona's," Albertina's dad said when he answered the phone. I've always loved Albertina's dad's voice. It's very deep and kind of rumbling. Right now, though, it sounded scratchy and a little worn out. I could tell things weren't going too well at their house, either.

"Mom, I'm going to go over to Mona's for a while," I said when I hung up.

"Is Sam locked up?" she asked.

"Yes, Mom." What fun is a pet if he's always locked away, I'd like to know.

Flynn opened the door when I got to Mona's. "Come on in," she said. "Mona and Albertina are upstairs."

"What am I going to do?" I asked when I walked into Mona's room. "They hate each other."

But Albertina had problems of her own, I realized when I took a look at her.

"Daddy's fighting with Sally," she said. "He actually yelled at her."

Now, some people's parents yell all the time. My mom is a yeller, for instance. Even my dad can get noisy if he's really upset. But Albertina's dad never yells. "Are you sure?" I asked.

"Molly, don't you think I'd know if my own father yelled?" She sounded pretty upset.

"Sorry," I mumbled. "Why are they fighting?"

"Daddy told Sally Duke can't stay with us. And Sally is supposed to leave tomorrow and now she doesn't have anyplace for Duke to go. She says he'd die of a broken heart in a kennel. So she's crying, and Daddy feels guilty, and I feel awful."

"I'm sure Flynn wouldn't mind taking him," Mona said, "but Creeps would go nuts. Besides, can you imagine Flynn trying to exercise the birds with a dog yapping away? How about you, Molly? Could you take him?"

Albertina looked at me hopefully. "Duke loves you, Molly."

I shook my head. "I'm in enough trouble already. Can you imagine my dad with Sam *and* Duke?"

All of a sudden I looked at Albertina, and she looked at me, and then we both looked at Mona.

We nodded as one. It was freaky. We were all thinking the same thing, and we could tell.

Mona spoke first. "Trading animals?"

"Yes!" We jumped up and ran downstairs.

"Good-bye, girls," Flynn called after us.

"How do we do this?" Albertina asked.

"We'll go get Duke and take him for a walk to my house," I said. "We'll have Dad and Mom come outside to meet him, and we'll explain the plan. Then, if they agree, we'll go back to your house and talk to your dad."

Albertina threw her arms around me. "Dad will agree to anything if it gets him out of trouble with Sally and still gets rid of Duke. I just know it. I'll take wonderful care of Sam! I'll have a cat at last!"

"For a while, Albertina," I reminded her. "I only get Duke for a month, remember."

"I know," she said. "But a month of joy is better than no joy at all."

## Chapter 15

# Surprise

"Please, Mom, Dad. It'll work. Albertina and I will make it work, and Mona will help, too."

It took some serious talking to get my parents to agree to the plan. It helped that Dad was so eager to get rid of Sam. Then we had to convince Albertina's dad to take Sam. It helped that *he* felt so guilty about not keeping Duke. Sally was the one person on our side from the start, since the only other alternative for Duke was the kennel.

It was definitely a month to remember. Duke was even more trouble than I expected, but I didn't mind, and Dad thought he was a lot better than Sam. Flynn came over to give me some tips on how to work with Duke, and my friends helped out, too. Albertina, Mona, and I repaired the backyard fence, with a little assistance from Dad, and Duke stayed back there when I was at school. Dad and Walter even took him to the park sometimes. By the time Sally came back, I had taught Duke to heel, at least most of the time, and to sit and shake hands.

Sally came to the house with Albertina and her dad.

"You're amazing," she said when I showed her what Duke could do. She gave me a big hug. "You should be an animal trainer." Duke looked gloriously happy to see her, and he wiggled in joy as she hugged him. Then she hugged me again. She even hugged Albertina's dad, but they didn't get married. Albertina didn't mind at all.

It *had* been a month of pure joy for Albertina. Sam was everything she'd ever dreamed of. Sam seemed pretty happy, too. You would have thought he was a dog, the way he followed her around the house.

"I'll go get Sam and bring him back," Albertina said after Sally and Duke left. I could tell she was trying not to cry.

I had a decision to make—a hard one. Albertina's dad didn't love Sam —but he liked him a lot more than my dad did! Sam definitely fit in at their house a lot better than he did at ours. Besides, even though I was very fond of Sam, I could tell that Sam was fonder of Albertina than he was of me. I took a big breath. "Sam belongs with you, Albertina," I said. "If your dad says it's okay." Now I was trying not to cry.

"Do you mean it?" She looked at me, and then she looked at her dad. He nodded. She jumped into his arms just like little kids do. "Thank you, thank you, thank you."

"It's Molly you need to thank," he said. His voice had returned to its relaxed, rumbling sound. He looked at me. "You are a very good friend, Molly."

I felt sad, but I knew it was the right thing. Albertina *and* my dad were both happy beyond words. They're two of my favorite people, so I couldn't feel too sorry for myself.

"I never thought things would turn out this way. Did you?" Albertina asked. I shook my head. I didn't feel like talking.

I went to the tree house after Albertina and

her dad left. Everybody had a happy ending, except me. I was back where I'd started. Saturday stretched out long and lonely.

When I went in the house for dinner, I felt empty. I missed Duke running to greet me the minute he heard my hand on the door. Then I reminded myself how happy he'd been to see Sally. I knew he was where he belonged, too.

It was a pretty quiet dinner until the doorbell rang. "I'll go," said Mom.

"It's Mona and her mom," she called from the living room. "Come here, everybody."

I followed Dad and Walter. Mona had her arms full of something wonderful.

"She's the friendliest dog in town," she said with a big smile.

Dad made a face. "Where have I heard this before?" he asked. But he wasn't really surprised. Mona had found the puppy at the pound, and

she and her mom had
talked to my parents
about him. While I
was out in the tree
house, Dad had
gone to the
pound and
signed the
papers.

"I know animals," Flynn said, "and I know you, Molly. You took great care of Duke—a big job for anybody. Your parents agree that you're ready for a dog of your own."

I didn't know what to say. Mona put the fuzzy pup in my arms. She was speckled, with big, floppy ears. Walter squealed. The puppy yapped. Albertina showed up and we all squealed, just like Walter.

I looked at Albertina, her face shining with the same happiness I felt. A little over a month ago, we were each wishing for just what we had now. It was amazing.

"What will you name her?" Mona asked. "You could call her Fortune Cookie, since that's where this all began."

I shook my head. "Remember *your* fortune cookie, Mom?" I asked.

"As a matter of fact, I do," Mom said. "Trouble is on the way." She laughed. "That fortune certainly came true."

I grinned at Albertina. "She *was* on the way. We just didn't know it."

"Who was?" Mom asked.

"Trouble," Albertina and I said, at the very same time. And Trouble wagged her tail.